KIERAN MCLOUGHLIN

Guardians of Odia: The Sacrifice

The Sacrifice

Contents

Acknowledgments

As always, I'd like to thank my family and those who have been part of my journey. None of this would've been possible without you. I'd also like to thank Christine and Jonathan for the editing, helping me make this novella the best it could be. Maxim, for the awesome cover design! All my beta readers, Immaculate, Nicholas, Scott, Marcie and Sumbul. You guys all provided amazing feedback which helped me shape this into what I wanted it to be. Finally, to you, my dear reader. I treasure each and every single one of you. Thank you for supporting my work.

1

Wrath

Tzui listened to the shrieks of the Infested as they drew closer, while the lifeless bodies of those who once had been of his kind surrounded him. He stared towards each of them, recognising his failure as a protector who hadn't protected his kind. The monsters' shrieking intensified as they approached, and he was sure that he could understand them now, sensing the emotions that were urging the beasts forward. He understood those voices because they reminded him of what he had become: a vessel who shared those very instincts. The Odian who harboured the very Infestation that was tearing his world apart.

This isn't what I'm supposed to be. Tzui thought, glancing towards Iri. Her chest bore a vast hole.

'Odians are supposed to protect the innocent!' he recalled her having said once, filling him with shame. Tzui remembered Fyr echoing a similar view. The Elder lay near Iri, as lifeless and dead as everybody else. No sooner did Tzui try to recall what had happened to them his thoughts became blurred, foggy. A fogginess that he guessed was coming from the Infestation

inside of him.

The Infestation now coursing through my veins...

What followed was an agonising strain in his mind, causing him to drop to one knee while he reached towards his head. Tzui squeezed it, hoping that the pressure would take away the pain. Certainty rose that something inside wished to take him over, whispering, laughing, and shrieking while threatening to send him towards madness. The Infestation sensed his presence, revealing its fear of him. It wished to destroy him, to remove what it perceived to be a threat to its survival. The Infestation recognised what he now was: a living manifestation of its own power. Yet, Tzui didn't want to relish this new body or its power. Instead, he found himself preoccupied with the bodies that surrounded him – the bodies of Iri, Fyr, his father, and the others.

'Sacrifice. All great things need sacrifice... he recalled his father saying, though he wasn't entirely sure why.

What did you mean, Father? What happened? Why is everybody dead?

Tzui lowered his hands before squeezing his fists, his body convulsing with rage for reasons he couldn't fathom.

What's going on? he wondered, recalling the journey that his kind had taken to wake their guardian, their Odian. Tzui understood now that he had become their Odian. He just couldn't remember how.

More shrieks emerged from the patch of overgrowth ahead. They were coming, rushing like a horde of insects.

You were the end of us, Tzui remembered, his determination strengthening. *Now, I will be the end of you...*

Hatred rose from within, while more of his new senses urged him to move faster. Voices murmured in his mind, incoherent and hateful

Kill!

Destroy!

Consume!

Tzui fought to keep control of his Infestation, knowing that he could force his will upon it at any moment. Wishing to distract himself from such thoughts, he peered towards a small patch of blue sky through the overgrowth that populated most of his world. Majestic trees and blooming plants intermingled with the thick tendrils that had spread across the planet, their spores covering everything like pollen. They made the contrasting neon glow of the plant life appear peaceful and wondrous.

'I am supposed to be a protector?' Tzui said, taking a couple of staggered steps. 'What am I supposed to protect now? Them?'

The thought filled him with disgust. No, he wouldn't protect them. He would make them pay for what they had forced him to become.

'But how did I become the Odian? How have I grown?' Tzui said, gazing towards his fists. They were larger than his Rakshian hands had been, while his body was now composed of a deep-black biological armour crossed with lines of crimson veins. Its texture was akin to that of the Infestation that was enveloping his world. However, unlike the Infestation's usual form, which varied in shape and size and was often asymmetrical, Tzui's body was sleek and even in build. Taking a moment to gaze upon his transformed body, Tzui saw that the crimson veins looked like fissures in cracked soil. He almost ran his fingers across them, to determine what they were and what purpose they served. Distracted by this, he found himself taken in by something he hadn't expected to see again, a neon crimson glow coupled with black that filled him with shame.

'Father's sword…'

His eyes fixed upon it as though it were one of the Infested. The weapon's hilt and blade were of the same black as his body, while its glowing neon crimson blade gleamed with an alluring haze. It was covered in tiny violet spores, pulsing as though alive.

Is it even possible for a sword to live? Tzui wondered, only realising that he was reaching towards it when his fingers brushed the hilt. He froze, his awe turning into repulsion.

Why? Why am I drawn to it? Why do I feel hatred towards it at the same time?

Tzui realised at that moment that part of the blade's hilt had lurched towards his outstretched hand, extending tiny tendrils of black Infestation that pulled it into his grasp. Jolting from a minor shock that accompanied an immediate sense of power, Tzui threw back his head and emitted his own horrifying shriek. A chorus of shrieks welcomed him in the distance. They were close.

No! I will not become one of you!

The sword tightened its grip around his fist, compelling Tzui to fling his arm in a series of wild arcs. He realised within seconds that his efforts were achieving nothing. This fuelled the sense of claustrophobia. The overgrowth seemed to draw in closer.

I can't get out! Tzui thought, panic rising as the futility of his movements fuelled his anger. The Infestation surged within him once again, gurging him forward, driving him towards the incoming horde.

We will crush them! his inner voice cried, fuelling his hate. *We will tear them limb from limb!*

'Yes…' Tzui said, allowing a grin to rise on his face beneath his armour. He knew it was his own Infestation urging him, pushing him further towards hatred. 'We will eradicate them…'

He heard them drawing closer, which added more fuel to his own impulsive desires. The ground trembled beneath his feet.

I can feel it. he realised, reaching a patch of thick overgrowth that separated him from the horde thundering towards him. *I feel you… Your pain. Your anguish. Your hatred. I understand what compels you, what commands your every step… But I refuse to accept remorse or pity for what I am going to do. It is because of you that I've lost everything. Everyone I ever loved. Everyone I ever treasured. They're gone… Replaced by the monster that I'm becoming, the lie that is the Odians. We are not the guardians of this universe. We are not heroes. No; we are the very thing we fear and despise most… And now, my dear Infestation, I own your power…*

Tzui raised his father's sword, which was still attached to his hand. Growling, he hacked through the overgrowth, relentless in his movement, unstoppable in his fury. He watched the vegetation recoil and shrink away from him, showing that he was the source of its suffering. Tzui hated himself for that, considering the pain he was inflicting upon his own world by doing what he was doing. Part of him wanted to stop.

No, I will not stop. The Infestation is the true enemy. It's turning us into monsters. I will destroy them no matter the cost!

'I will kill you all!'

Tzui broke through the last recoiling tendril, emerging into a rare patch of open space. Prowling forward with his father's sword at the ready, he held out his arms and shouted, 'Every one of you!'

He moved to continue on his path of destruction, but his body stopped, unable to proceed. As he strained forward, it felt as though something had attached itself to him, keeping him from advancing. Scowling as he looked over his shoulder, he saw that many little black tendrils had emerged from his back, reaching into the overgrowth and attaching themselves to it. They were repairing the damage he had caused, then breaking off and returning to him once they were done. This lasted a couple of seconds, leaving the overgrowth repaired with patches of Infestation.

'What is this?' he said, his anger dissipating while his confusion intensified. Tzui glanced at his new body again, discovering something else that amazed him just as much. Across his skin he saw many cuts; battling through the overgrowth must have inflicted them upon him. Yet, just as his body had repaired the overgrowth, it also had moved to repair itself with Infestation. His skin-like armour crawled as though it possessed a parasite. Within a few seconds he found his body completely healed, leaving him stunned.

'Can I self-regenerate?' Tzui asked. What astonished him was that his mouth had stated that term having never done so before, although he understood what it meant. Rakshians never used such terms, so why he was using it now mystified him as much as the power he was manifesting.

'The Infestation... It's only meant to destroy...' he said, glancing between his body and the overgrowth behind him and finding something else entirely.

'What is happening?'

A single Infested emerged from the other side of the clearing, landing with a crash and a tumble, which drew his attention towards it. It was a bizarre-looking creature. They all were. Its body, possessing four mismatched asymmetrical limbs, appeared as though it had originated from the overgrowth itself. Its colour was a deep burgundy, dotted with neon growths that glowed green and yellow. Its face was grotesque, appearing half-complete, deformed, and hateful. It looked like two very different creatures meshed into one, both sharing a similar purpose as it shrieked. It wanted to kill him, to destroy him and change him into one of its own. Tzui guessed it didn't realise that he was one of them now, while just seeing the creature threatened to unleash his anger once again. His own confusion was inescapable, forcing him to glance back and forth between the monster and the overgrowth while frowning.

'The Infestation can destroy and heal?' Tzui asked, his bewilderment and anger tearing at him while his inner Infestation urged him towards rage and hatred.

DESTROY THEM! it screamed as he raised his sword, his conviction still waning. More monsters burst from the overgrowth to join the first, as Tzui held himself still.

'Why would it heal my world if it sought to destroy it?' Tzui asked again, before his mind began filling with new images, pictures of his kind lying dead. He recalled seeing tendrils pulling away from them, slithering as they returned to him. He remembered…

What do I remember? Tzui wondered, the fog returning to cloud his mind. Before him, the Infested sounded their shrieks and their hateful roars, causing Tzui to stand, unsure of what to do.

What happened to me?

He only realised that the slits across his body had opened when he returned his gaze to the Infested and black tendrils emerging from him appeared in his field of vision. The monsters saw them and backed away, terrified.

'You should fear me', he said, allowing gratification to surface despite his confusion, 'I am the monster you created.'

Tzui stopped then, as a memory emerged from the fog in his mind.

2

Questions

Tzui recalled times before the Infested – simple times when the most his kind had needed to deal with were the likes of the Tshunus and the Liagnis. Tshunus were rainbow-fleeced catlike beasts with sharp fangs and claws, while Liagnis were flying reptilian creatures that swept from the trees, carrying victims away to their nests. One could avoid these, so long as one travelled with a group. It was only when hunting the creatures that his people had been likely to lose someone. Tzui remembered this.

And he also remembered the day the horde had come.

Hearing roars and shrieks emerging from somewhere in the north, his kind had known something was wrong. His father left at once to investigate, taking a few of his greatest warriors with him. They returned half in number and covered with deep wounds. To show for it, his father carried a strange glowing black sword, a weapon Tzui had never seen before. Despite his kinds growing fear, they had approached his father, concerned about the fate of the others. His father had elected to say nothing to their questions, instead speaking words of command.

'We must go to the temple of our Odian. We must wake it…'

Tzui had never heard of his planet's guardian before. He wondered if it would look like his father, a tall, muscular Rakshian with light-blue skin and yellow eyes, his head shaped like a raindrop. He also imagined other forms, forms that looked more like the creatures that lived amongst them, hybrids of Tshunus and Liagnis. Of course, his father refused to entertain such ideas. He refused to explain what had happened during the first encounter with the Infested. Tzui had pretended to be asleep to learn this, eavesdropping as his father revealed the truth to the Elders during the first night of their pilgrimage to the temple.

'They are a horde, an Infestation,' his father had begun. 'Terrifying beasts that spread disease wherever they touch, changing everything into one of them, filling them with rage and frenzy. Fuelled by this rage when they saw us, they came bounding, roaring, and shrieking. We fought, but they kept coming, like a stampede of enraged Alphus. We realised we couldn't hold them back – I mean, if it weren't for the sacrifices of…'

His father trailed off, showing a rare gesture of disappointment, regret, and shame. Such emotions sent a haunting shiver through Tzui, causing his eyes to widen. He waited for someone to ask his father a question about his sword, but no one uttered a word about it. The group continued on their pilgrimage the next day as though nothing had happened, progressing towards the temple where their Odian rested.

Dread followed their every step. Often, they heard the roars and shrieks of the monsters pursuing them. Days soon passed. No sign of the temple appeared, while his father still refused to answer any of Tzui's questions about it. His frustration growing, Tzui decided one night to ask the one Rakshian who might entertain his queries: the Elder known as Fyr.

Fyr was the oldest Rakshian of their village, the Elder who had been leader before his father. Most days, he would tell stories to the likes of Tzui and the other children. Fyr was a master at storytelling, weaving enchanting tales with mystical lore and fantasies until their minds spun. It was the reason they loved him. In a journey so bleak and full of anxiety, he smiled while promising them better days, regaling them with the exploits of heroes and legends.

Tzui waited until Fyr was in the middle of recounting one of his stories before deciding to ask his most burning question, raising his hand to interrupt him.

'Fyr, what are the Odians?'

As Tzui had expected, no sooner had the words left his lips than the other children fell silent. He didn't doubt they had been wondering the same thing, never daring to ask Fyr themselves. He used this to buffer his courage. Keeping himself tall, Tzui even risked a glimpse towards Iri, who was smiling in amusement coupled with admiration. Tzui only smiled back, finding more courage as he forced his gaze towards Fyr, unsurprised to see a bemused twinkle in his eye.

'I have been waiting for someone to ask that,' Fyr said, his words, as always, carrying authority. 'Should it surprise me that young Tzui was the first to speak?'

Tzui hesitated. Under the Elder's gaze, he couldn't help but fluster. Fyr was a dignified man, one whom Tzui guessed had been as powerful as his father, now wrinkled with age, with a wispy white beard and a stooping posture.

'I assume that this question resides within you all?' Fyr

continued.

The children nodded, as though waiting for the Elder to pull the Alphu skin out from underneath them. Fyr shook his head as a smile appeared on his lips. Tzui could see Loya Flies hovering near the Elder, shinning a majestic silvery light that contrasted with the glowing neon colours of the tendrils and overgrowth. Because of them, Tzui became distracted.

'Very well, my dear children,' Fyr said, drawing Tzui's attention back to him. 'I shall tell to you the legends of the Odians...'

He gestured for the group to draw closer, urging the children forward. They glanced up, looking at him as though he were about to tell his greatest tale yet. The Elder began by holding out his arms and waving them in dramatic fashion. As Tzui cast his gaze over the other children, he could feel the respect they held for Fyr. He was a Rakshian like no other.

'The Odians are the guardians who protect all living things in the Odia Universe,' Fyr started, raising a hand towards the sky. 'The ones who protect us from the Anubians—'

At once, the children thrust their hands into the air.

'What are the Anubians?'

'What is the Odia Universe?'

'Why is ours in a temple?' a third asked, prompting a few more concerned looks to emerge. No other question followed, and Tzui remained silent, also wishing to know the answer. The third child gazed in the others' direction, hesitant. He gulped before returning his focus to Fyr, appearing afraid to utter what hung at the back of his throat.

'What I mean—' he began.

'I know what you mean, young Obo,' Fyr said, silencing him. 'What you are asking is why our protector hasn't emerged yet. You wonder why we travel to the temple, when none of us have ever spoken of it, nor of our protector. You wonder why it hasn't emerged to meet the Infested...'

Fyr gazed towards the other children then, his smile growing.

'Oh, was I not supposed to mention them? Was I meant to pretend that none of you were listening to Kyri's explanation of what happened – that you were sleeping like good little children?'

They all looked away, saying nothing. It took a joyful laugh from the Elder to regain their attention; they watched as he rose to his feet and held up his staff below the glowing canopy.

'Do you see this?' he asked. The children didn't answer. Even Iri, so forward and direct with her precise questions, said nothing. To them, it was a rhetorical question. Fyr confirmed this a few seconds later, gesturing with his other hand at the glowing trees of overgrowth behind them.

'Do you see this?' he asked again, his voice growing in grandeur. 'Our home, where our kind and many other wonderful creatures live together in harmony!'

He paused for a moment, revealing to the children a rare gravity of expression.

'Yet, many other worlds are out there. Some like Rakshi. Some not. What unites us is that we exist within the Odia Universe. It is vast and wondrous, a place of planets, stars, and gods!'

He smiled before sitting back on the glowing pink tendril he'd chosen for his seat, calming before he spoke again.

'The Odians... Their task is to protect us from the corruption that threatens to ruin all things – the corruption that comes from their mortal enemies. The Anubians...'

Fyr paused, giving them time to comprehend his words. Because of this, none of the children raised their hand. Even

Tzui felt stunned by his words. He saw the beginnings of a smile curling on the Elder's lips, a sign that he hadn't said everything yet. As was often the case with Fyr, more lay beneath the words he had spoken.

'My dear children… Odia gave us a wonderful gift. The fact that we exist in this moment is a miracle! Yet, the corruption can still ruin us. The Anubians – they seek to twist and bend the minds of those who wish to live in peace. Because of this, Odia blessed us with her guardians, the Odians. It is their duty to protect. The Anubians – they seek to unleash corruption, turning everything into monsters…'

'Like the Infested,' Tzui said aloud. It drew everyone's attention to him. Fyr appeared to consider his words, then spoke again.

'Perhaps,' the Elder said. 'But I do not believe that the Infested are monsters…'

'How do you know that?' Iri said, unable to hide her incredulousness and agitation.

Despite her harsh tone, Fyr appeared unfazed by her challenge. He stared at her as though she were nothing more than an innocent child, barely touching upon what he knew. He held her gaze in a long pause, his smile slowly returning to his lips.

'My dear Iri,' he began. 'As much as I know this may frustrate you, there are things that you are too young to understand. Please, do not mistake this for insult. Sometimes, only time can give you answers. Remember, wisdom can only be attained by those who can gaze back upon their past and recognise their mistakes. It is because of this that I am afraid I cannot answer your question, my young Iri.'

Satisfied with his own answer, he shifted his eyes to Tzui, regarding him with a knowing smirk. 'So, you have a question concerning the Infested?' Fyr asked.

'I—' Tzui started to reply, but his senses alerted him to the approach of another. Glancing behind, he realised his father was there, looking as though he'd been watching the whole time. He appeared expectant, his powerful arms folded across his chest. Despite this, Tzui's gaze was drawn to the glowing sword tied to his father's waist, burning a radiant crimson.

'I—' Tzui tried to speak again, but an unusual sensation arose within him. It was as though the sword was urging him to approach. It was so surprising that Tzui lost his original thoughts, his lips parting while his eyes refused to be drawn away from the elegant weapon.

'Tzui,' his father said, snapping the weapon's hold over him. Fyr met Kyri's gaze. 'Elder Fyr asked you a question.'

Nodding, still enchanted by the sword, Tzui saw that Fyr was now standing on his feet, grasping his staff.

'Kyri,' Fyr said, 'may I have a couple of minutes with Tzui?'

'Of course, Elder Fyr,' Kyri responded with reverence. Tzui kept his gaze fixed upon Fyr, who was now staring at him with an unreadable expression.

'All of you, to sleep,' his father ordered the other children, leaving no room for dispute. The children rose to their feet, and Tzui allowed himself to glance towards Iri, who smiled at him before turning to leave. Soon, it was just him, Fyr, and his father standing, allowing an awkward silence to emerge before his father did something Tzui had never seen him do.

He bowed to Fyr.

'Take as long as you need, Elder Fyr,' he said, before taking another glance at Tzui. He then turned and followed the children out.

'Your father is a good man, young Tzui,' Fyr said, drawing

Tzui's attention back to him. 'Had the circumstances been different, I know he would've made a wise Elder.'

His eyes flickered towards Tzui.

'Right now, his task is difficult. Please forgive him if he's become short with you. He harbours great expectations of you, but his biggest wish is for you to survive.'

Fyr gestured to the space before him, compelling Tzui to acknowledge this before he took his place. The Elder sat on the glowing pink tendril, shifting his staff from one hand to the other.

'I've underestimated Iri's influence on you, young Tzui,' he said, his smile coming back. 'She has taught you to see beyond the words, to ask questions and consider everything you're told. Indeed, much like her questions, yours require a different answer.'

He paused, as though gauging Tzui's response. Tzui said nothing, trying to fix the Elder with a measured gaze. This drew from Fyr an amused one in return.

'So, young Tzui, you wish to discuss the horde that pursues us,' he said.

3

Monster

'Let me ask you something, young Tzui,' the Elder began, allowing his gaze to drift up toward the glowing canopy, pondering. 'What do you think the Infested are?'

Tzui frowned at the question, believing the answer was obvious. Yet despite his first thought, he kept his mouth shut, knowing that Fyr often liked to phrase questions that way to make someone think before they responded. There was always a layer beneath everything to Fyr. As a result, Tzui took a moment to consider the question, drawing a wry smile from the Elder, who appeared expectant yet patient. The problem with Fyr's expression was that it fuelled pressure in Tzui's mind, compelling him to glance away as he drew a hand towards his lips.

'Monsters,' he said, his confidence returning as he spoke the word. 'They're monsters that wish to destroy everything.'

'Are you sure?' Fyr asked.

'Well… Yeah…' Tzui was annoyed at himself for allowing his doubt to shine through. 'What else could they be? Even now we're running from them, struggling to find our Odian! What could they be except monsters?'

Fyr nodded without responding, a satisfied but contemplative look on his face.

'I see…' he said. 'Let me ask you something, then. Let us assume that your point of view is correct and that the Infested are indeed monsters. What, then, makes something a monster?'

Tzui's frustration grew; he believed this to be another question with a straightforward answer.

'Monsters destroy things—' He tried to control himself. 'The Infested want to hurt others. They infect things. They turn things into one of them. If they aren't monsters, then why are we running away from them?!'

This mild outburst drew Fyr's smile once again, as though he considered it as naïve as he perceived Tzui to be.

At once, Tzui rose to his feet, clenching his fists. 'Why can't you say what you want to say?! Why do you ask these foolish questions?!'

Tzui felt shame as the words left his lips; he glanced behind him to see if his tantrum had woken any of the others. No one appeared to have stirred, but he remembered the trick he and other children had attempted. It wouldn't surprise him if everyone was listening to them right now. He forced himself to relax, bowing in apology to Fyr.

'I'm sorry, Elder Fyr,' he said, casting his gaze towards the floor.

'Young Tzui,' Fyr said, drawing Tzui's gaze back to him while gesturing for him to take his seat before him once more. Tzui did so. 'Have you ever thought that the best way to help someone understand your view might be to help them arrive at it themself? Have you ever considered that the best way to answer a question might be by asking another?'

Tzui said nothing. He knew the Elder had no intention of letting him respond. He watched as Fyr raised his staff high in the air, gesturing once more at the glowing canopy above them.

'As you know, young Tzui, if one looked towards the trees above for long enough, one might see the majestic sight of a Liagni. Or if one searched within the overgrowth, one might even stumble across a family of Alphus. Yet I wonder… Do you ever think that they might watch us, as we build our settlements and hunt their loved ones? That they might think of us as "monsters"?'

Tzui frowned again, confused.

'But we're nothing like them…' he said, doubting himself. 'From what Father said, the Infested are just mindless beasts. How could you even compare us to them?'

'And what if we decide to move village, young Tzui?' Fyr replied. 'Or what if we seek better hunting spots? Do you think these things are any different from what the Infested could be trying to achieve? Are we truly any different, when you consider *their* perspective?'

Tzui opened his mouth to respond but found himself incapable of speaking, unsure of what to say. Fyr remained silent, patient, as though prompting him to seek further within himself for something, for a truth Tzui wasn't sure he could figure out.

'If one cannot consider the thoughts and feelings of another, how can one understand the thoughts and feelings of oneself?' the Elder said. Tzui froze, contemplating the words.

Why is he confusing me? Tzui wondered, new emotions swelling within him. Stunned, he couldn't help but place a hand over his chest.

'You feel it, don't you?' Fyr asked, snapping Tzui's attention back to him. 'You feel your soul burning with truth. The internal force has risen within you. Do not turn it away. Let it envelop you. Let it help you become who you are supposed to be.'

'What do you mean?' Tzui asked. 'I don't understand...'

The Elder smiled.

'Do not fear what you are, young Tzui... You are capable of compassion. It is part of the reason you are here. You seek to understand, to find the truth beyond what your mind sees. This is who you are, who you are supposed to be. Do not fear this. Do not fear what stirs in your heart...'

In a move Tzui was not expecting, the Elder leaned towards him.

'You must undergo the test. We must see if my intuition is correct. We must see if he was right all those years ago. I will speak with your father. Now, time you went to sleep, young Tzui. Tomorrow, we continue on our journey...'

Tzui didn't want to leave and was unable to escape his confusion. Even though he was disappointed, he rose to his feet, regarding the Elder with a sad expression.

'I still don't understand,' he said.

'Do not fear your lack of understanding,' Fyr answered. 'Only ask yourself this. If the Infested are monsters, what does that make us?'

Moving away to join the others, Tzui pondered that, the sensation Fyr had described still bubbling within him. He closed his eyes and tried to listen to it, hearing it pulse while another new feeling arose inside him. Tzui's gaze hovered upon his people, then he was surprised to find it drawn towards his father, to the sword that hung on his waist.

There's something about that sword, he realised, fighting to ensure he didn't show his shock. Then an answer came to him, compelling him to return his gaze to Fyr.

'The Infested are monsters,' he said, uttering the answer with a sense of finality. Much to his surprise, the Elder nodded in agreement.

'They are indeed, young Tzui,' he said. 'But so are we. The mistake you made was in thinking that we are not...'

Tzui returned to himself as the conversation ended in his mind. Seeing piles of dead Infested bodies surrounding him, he realised he had lost himself again. Lowering his sword, he felt an eeriness that came with realising they looked the same as his kind had looked to him when he had first awoken as his world's Odian. He also felt something emerging from within, battling the impulses that screamed at him to continue his assault.

Destroy them! his inner voice howled. *Show them no mercy!*

Tzui remained still, watching as the horde retreated, roaring and shrieking at him. He took advantage of the moment to examine the bloodshed he had inflicted. He could see the monsters he had carved with his father's sword alongside those his own body had killed by itself. Indeed, he could see many tendrils that had emerged from the crimson slits in his body, attached to the dying as they drained them, filling him with life.

What am I doing? Tzui asked himself, taking a deep breath as something shifted in the overgrowth. Something was coming, something big. His instincts compelled him to raise his father's sword, and he watched as the horde parted, making room.

They took everything from you, his inner voice whispered. *They've ravaged and ruined your beautiful world...They deserve this. They deserve punishment!*

'Yes, they do... Tendra...' Tzui said, the word of command leaving his lips despite him not thinking of it until that moment.

He wasn't sure why. His tendrils, responding, snapped away from the dead bodies and returned to him, rising as though he now possessed vastly more arms, ready to strike and absorb life from whatever they struck.

Yet, they repaired, too, Tzui remembered. *They healed.*

Before he could consider that further, three more of the Infested launched themselves towards him. His body, reacting as though it possessed its own will, sliced the first attacker in half. His tendrils rushed to take the other two, pinning them at either side. His body seemed to revel in its new prey, yearning for the lives of the two creatures who lay powerless as it drained them. The monsters who had stayed back shrieked, spitting an acidic bile that burned his armour, generating smoke. Yet, none of this fazed him in the least. They were no match for him. He was now an Odian.

Compulsion urging him forward, Tzui strode to meet them, slaughtering all that threw themselves at him. As he did so, a rustling of overgrowth unveiled two new Infested beasts, larger monsters with sizeable guts, dragging themselves along the ground. At their emergence, the others moved away, regarding Tzui with hatred as they sounded their awful shrieks.

Use me... his inner voice growled inside of him, drawing him towards the enemy as he placed the sword near his side. A series of tiny tendrils emerged from his body, fixing the sword against him. After doing this, Tzui noticed a shifting sensation in his forearms; it looked as though a parasite lurked beneath his skin, longing to be unleashed. His instincts compelled him towards his own hatred and he recalled the images of all his kind lying dead around him.

You turned me into this. You made me a monster...

'For my kind...' he sneered, instinctively plunging his hands into the surface.

'Infest!'

At once his forearms hardened, pulling him farther into the ground while he remained attached. Driven by compulsion and instinct alone, he sounded his own terrifying shriek, jerking as he strained to pull himself free. Yet his arms didn't give way, summoning power from within while travelling beneath, pulling him to the large Infested that continued to shift towards him.

'I will not allow you to ruin another world.' He grunted, jerking his arms once more. This time he pulled them free with a snapping sound followed by a sudden outburst of towering spikes. The spikes drove through the two large Infested, lofting them into the air and impaling them high on the overgrowth – one on a tree and one on a thick tendril. Witnessing this, the surrounding horde fell into a horrified silence, gazing up at their impaled champions and watching as violet blood trickled from the spikes. At the sight of this new power, Tzui grinned with elation. They were nothing to him. They were no match for the power of an Odian.

'I smell your fear,' he said, then realised he'd spoken in perfect sync with the voice inside his head. 'You will pay for what you've done!'

Tzui heard another sound emerge from high above, and he froze. Above the canopy, he saw a majestic Liagni gliding in the air, the folds of excess skin under the yellow reptile's arms stretched taut to keep it aloft. Watching as it circled while it emitted its customary screech, Tzui couldn't help but become transfixed by it.

'I thought they would've destroyed you by now,' he said, amazed. 'Yet, some of you still live...'

The memory of Fyr returned to him, reminding him of the conversation they had shared that night.

'As you know, young Tzui, if one looked towards the trees above for long enough, one might see the majestic sight of a Liagni. Or if one searched within the overgrowth, one might even stumble across a family of Alphus. Yet I wonder... Do you ever think that they might watch us, as we build our settlements and hunt their loved ones? That they might think of us as "monsters"?'

I want to protect them, Tzui thought, as the sensation returned from within, faint though it was. A part of him felt he'd once understood what it meant, but now he couldn't remember.

'I've only just become an Odian,' he said. 'How did I forget?'

Tzui searched his mind, finding nothing but an empty void, which he felt should have contained memories. Yet, the earliest thing he could remember was his conversation with Fyr before he'd awoken as his world's protector, surrounded by his own kind.

'Sacrifice. All great things require sacrifice,' he remembered his father saying, adding to his confusion.

There was a sacrifice. He strained to think, trying to remember. *That's why I'm the Odian. I'm sure of it. Yet, why have I forgotten everything? Why do I feel this fog in my mind?*

He returned his attention to the horde, which now appeared reluctant to meet him, seeing something that he realised should have been obvious. They trembled in fear, inching towards those he had slaughtered, appearing heartbroken by their deaths.

'They are monsters...' He remembered saying to Fyr, despite now witnessing something different. Tzui moved a step forward, drawing another hateful shriek from the horde. He glanced towards the canopy once more, watching the Liagni

that continued to circle high above.

Liagnis... When their nests are threatened, they act aggressively. They try to drive you away...

His eyes widened within his armour, realising something as he stopped.

You're protecting something...

The familiar sensation emerged again. It came from somewhere beyond his instincts. It pulsed more now, as though he were reaching towards it and it was responding to him.

'Is that why you've been chasing us?' he asked. 'Is that why you've been attacking? All this time, were you protecting something?'

It doesn't matter, his inner voice said, threatening to cut the tie Tzui had to the familiar pulsing inside of him. *Kill them.*

'No. Wait a second.' Tzui felt as though he were arguing with a part of himself. 'There's something more to this… Something I'm…'

His head throbbed in pain, trying to remember.

Do not become weak, his inner voice said. *If you do not fight, then you shall never learn the truth. You will never learn why everyone you loved had to die...*

'But how do you know?' he asked. 'Aren't you… me?'

His inner voice didn't respond. The familiar sensation from within grew, as though the more he thought the stronger it became. Tzui tried to search his memories, to find something that could explain what had happened.

'There's more to this.' He returned his gaze to the horde. 'I'm missing something. What happened to me? I'm supposed to be an Odian, a protector of the universe.'

He recalled Fyr's words about the Odians and their greatest foes.

'The Anubians… The corruption.' He gawked, finding himself gazing at his body. 'Is that what's happening to me? Am I becoming corrupted?'

His inner voice grumbled inside, and another memory returned to him.

Of Iri.

4

Iri

It had been the day after his conversation with Fyr, when Tzui was walking alongside Iri as they trailed behind the group. Tzui remembered wondering if the pilgrimage would last the rest of their lives, and hearing occasional shrieks and roars in the distance that seemed to answer the question for him. There were only two ways this journey could end – either they would find their Odian, or the Infested would catch them. This hollowing thought kept him silent, considering every word he and Fyr had shared that night.

It was an easy silence to maintain with Iri alongside him. She was one of the rare few he could find comfort sharing quiet with, never needing to fill the air with meaningless conversation. Instead, Tzui chose to remain within his thoughts, casting a glance at Iri as she held out her arm, trickling her fingers through the overgrowth. Iri cherished their world, and Tzui cherished her. He guessed she knew that. Women seemed to possess a secret intuition for those things on Rakshi. Tzui was thankful that he didn't make their relationship awkward. Besides, he was perhaps the only Rakshian in their village who could entertain her 'challenging side', as an Elder had described it.

Even that was another reason he adored her. He admired her strength, passion, and determination. Iri continuously frustrated the adults and Elders by questioning them, then proceeding to debate their answers. This was especially true for those who tried to avoid her questions. They were the ones who often endured the full might of 'Iri's tongue', as Fyr had coined it a few years ago, laughing while doing so.

'Surely,' she began, drawing Tzui's attention and looking upon him with an amused expression, 'they can see how wonderful our planet is? Surely, they can sense we mean no harm to them?'

Tzui opened his mouth to speak, knowing who she was referring to. Again, Fyr's words reduced him to a frustrated silence. Iri didn't speak, not moving to compel him to say anything. For all her boldness and her legendary tongue, she understood when not to push him. Tzui appreciated that, watching her as she continued to brush her fingers against the glowing tendrils and plants, which seemed to respond to her favourably as she touched them.

His peripheral vision caught a tiny flicker of movement in the overgrowth, freezing him in place. He prayed that it wasn't the Infested, and found instead a pair of innocent shiny blue eyes staring back at him, as though terrified of the same thing. He spun his gaze to make sure no one had noticed his pause. Tzui didn't doubt that Iri had. That was why he appreciated it when she walked along acting as though nothing had occurred, allowing him to return his attention to the overgrowth. With much relief, he saw the eyes had disappeared. Satisfied, Tzui briskly returned to Iri, hoping that to anyone else glancing towards them it appeared as though he had peed and was running to catch up to her.

'Alphus,' Iri whispered, without moving her gaze while making sure that no one ahead could hear them. Tzui nodded. Nothing else needed to be said.

'You remember you won't be able to protect them during the rite of passage?' she said, eliciting a regretful look from him that he hoped answered her question.

'I'm not sixteen,' he said. 'I still have another three years.'

Iri said nothing, for which Tzui was thankful. The conversation was at risk of drifting towards another topic that became important at the same age: marriage. He didn't doubt that she knew who he intended on proposing to. Still, he allowed the silence to return between them, his eyes dropping. Alphus were always part of the rite of passage, reminding Tzui of Fyr's words on how the other creatures must view his kind.

We are monsters, aren't we? Tzui pondered.

'There's something you're not telling me,' Iri said. 'You know I don't wish to force you to say anything…'

'Don't,' Tzui said, cringing from the harshness of his answer. That normally would be enough to earn a tongue-lashing from Iri. She didn't give one. Instead, she looked upon him with understanding. This only fuelled the sense of guilt building inside of him.

'Keeping it to yourself will not make you feel any better…' She reached out her left hand. Tzui froze, sure that she was going to touch him. However, Iri seemed to recognise what she was doing, pulling away as though she'd been inches away from touching flame. Both of them snapped their attention awkwardly forward as they continued to walk, pretending that hadn't happened.

'Fyr talked about them, didn't he?' Iri asked a couple of

minutes later, less questioning than seeking confirmation. For a moment Tzui contemplated how he could explain his confusion, the words he and the Elder had shared. Iri remained patient, holding her gaze upon him.

'Have you ever thought that the best way to answer a question is by asking another?' Tzui recalled, remembering Fyr's remarks.

'Do you think they're monsters, Iri?' he asked, watching her intently as she considered it.

'What do you think?' Iri asked in return. It was not the answer he wanted to hear.

'I don't know,' he lied, unsure why he had done so. 'That's what Elder Fyr and I discussed last night. He thinks we're… like them in some ways, but I don't understand how that can be true. Yet…'

'You see similarities,' Iri finished. Much to Tzui's disappointment, he nodded.

'Yes. Part of me wants to agree with him. Yet there's another part of me that believes there's a difference between us. I feel this… strange feeling inside of me, Iri. It's like another heartbeat, trying to speak to me in a language I do not know. Yet, I feel like I understand what it's saying to me.'

Tzui hesitated, realising he must've sounded as though he were experiencing delusions.

'You must think I'm hallucinating,' he said.

'No, I don't think so.' She regarded him in earnest. 'I've noticed that you keep staring at your father's sword, though.'

Tzui looked away in embarrassment. Had it been that obvious?

'I can feel it, Iri. I know that makes no sense.' He returned the gaze. 'But it feels like it wants to talk to me, to do something with me. I don't know how else to explain it.'

'Don't.' Iri smiled warmly. 'You'll figure it out. You always do.'

Tzui couldn't help but smile back, hoping that it conveyed his appreciation. For a couple of minutes they walked in silence again, while Tzui felt the peculiar sensation rising from within once more, causing him to frown.

'You can feel it now, can't you?' Iri asked.

'Yes.'

'What is it saying?'

That was, like so many of Iri's questions, a dangerous one. It was dangerous because it would force him to acknowledge the sensation directly, along with the words that came with it. This time, Tzui allowed himself to listen, closing his eyes as he walked. Inside, it sang a wonderful melody, radiant and happy. It was as though it felt grateful to be listened to, filling him with an enthusiasm that frightened and enthralled him in equal measure.

'I don't think they're monsters...' he said, opening his eyes as he tried to come to terms with it. 'I don't think they're just mindless beasts.'

'What are they, then?' Iri asked, sounding as though she was afraid of the answer herself.

'I don't know,' Tzui admitted. 'I can't tell what it's saying now.'

Iri nodded, appearing satisfied with that answer. She allowed herself to return her hand to the tendrils and overgrowth.

'Before, you said that you thought there was a difference between us and them. What was it?'

Tzui forced himself to search within again, this time not closing his eyes, as the answer arrived quickly.

'That we have a choice,' he said. He looked up to see his father approaching along with three of his most trusted warriors. His expression was grave.

'Tzui, come,' Kyri said. 'It is time for your rite of passage.'

For a moment, Tzui wondered if he had heard his father right. He stopped by Iri, casting a bewildered gaze.

'What do you mean?' he dared to ask, disliking how baffled he sounded. 'I am not sixteen.'

'Yes,' his father agreed, speaking as though this didn't matter in the slightest. 'But Elder Fyr has informed me you are to take the test. We must go now...'

Without hesitation, his father walked into the overgrowth to the right, his warriors following closely. Tzui cast a troubled yet sorrowful glance towards Iri, who appeared just as confused. Despite his reluctance, he lowered his gaze and caught up with the hunting party. Tzui's head was spinning with fear alongside confusion. His rite of passage was about to begin.

This is not meant to happen... Why now?

5

The Hunt

Tzui remembered running to keep up with his father, terrified of what was about to happen. The suddenness didn't help things either, especially now that he knew this was the test Fyr had meant earlier.

I'm not ready for this, he thought as his breathing quickened. *I'm not ready to kill Alphus...*

He scrambled to catch up, almost pleading for his father to explain why they were doing this. Yet, no sooner did he reach the group than his father turned to regard him, stifling any voice that threatened to emerge.

'Remember, Tzui, Alphus are vulnerable to surprise attacks. The closer you can get, the better. Watch.' His father and the other warriors crouched and stalked through the overgrowth, imitating the movement patterns of the beasts they were hunting. They spread into a crescent-shaped formation, Kyri in the centre with the others flanking him on either side. The warriors moved with effortless poise, navigating the overgrowth without making a sound. Tzui followed. They paused frequently, uttering unusual sounds, signalling something he didn't understand. All he could do was trail after them, his anxiety growing with each passing second. He was struggling to comprehend why this was happening, why they were doing this now during their pilgrimage.

An hour passed. Tzui did not know where they were. Indeed, part of him wondered how they would find the others. He knew such thoughts were foolish. They wouldn't be returning until the rite of passage was complete. Tzui remembered seeing rites of passage that had taken days before the warriors returned. In the meantime, the best he could do was move with them, trying to copy his father's steps.

Then the entire group stopped. His father stretched out an arm with a cautious gesture as a whistle sounded from the left, a whistle that looped from high to low. His father turned and regarded Tzui with a gentle expression, as though he could now drop an act he had been playing. Surprised to see this unusual turn from his father, Tzui moved towards him.

'They're close; stay behind me,' Kyri whispered. Tzui nodded, unsure of what to say. His father then returned his attention to the others, watching as they changed direction. They had been heading southeast for around fifty metres when Tzui heard a sound he recognised. It was a sound reminiscent of someone blowing their nose.

We've found them, Tzui realised, his stomach twisting as nausea rose. Oblivious, the formation proceeded, slowing its pace even more as the sound of the Alphus grew. They weren't moving; that much was obvious. Tzui recognised another sound among them, too, a gentler sound that made his heart twist in agony.

They have young.

He felt a sudden compulsion to burst out from their current position, or at least make an unusual noise to give the unsuspecting Alphus a chance to escape. He knew such an effort was useless. Young Alphus wouldn't be strong enough to run away from them.

Please, at least let them be in a herd, Tzui prayed. He looked up and saw his father regarding him with concern, prompting a jolt of panic.

'Are you alright, son?' his father asked, saying it in such a gentle way that Tzui frowned towards him.

What's happening to you? he almost asked.

'I… don't know if I can do this,' he said, but before his father could reply, another loud whistle emerged from their left. Before Tzui knew what was going on, his father moved, driven by instinct. He burst from the overgrowth into an open space where a small family of Alphus were resting. The animals, which hadn't sensed their presence, startled with panic and confusion, and a large male rose onto its legs, emitting a panicked snort from its stubby trunk. Two of Kyri's warriors, knowing that it was the greatest threat, plunged their spears deep into its gut and hind legs, making it groan as it fell. The second adult, the female, attempted to rise, still trying to figure out what was happening.

Tzui, erupting from the overgrowth, now understood why that strategy was so effective, watching as his father leapt towards the female and swung himself around by its neck. Tzui raised his hands and tried to utter a cry for him to stop. However, before any sound left his lips, his father unsheathed his glowing sword. Tzui stared for a moment in awe, before his father drew it across the female's throat, cutting it without a second of hesitation.

Tzui's awe snapped into horror at the sight of the killing, freezing him. Time slowed, his eyes falling upon the two remaining young Alphus, which found themselves trapped between his people and their parents, their blue eyes wide with terror.

We are monsters, he realised, remembering his conversation with Fyr and his thoughts with Iri. Without even realising what he was doing, he dashed for the young Alphus, compelled to move, compelled to act.

Compelled to protect.

Before he knew what was happening, he had fallen to his knees, using his entire body to shield the young Alphus. Trembling, he closed his eyes (now full of tears) and prepared himself for the spears to come down upon him. Yet, as he remained in his defensive posture, waiting for either the killing blow or for his father to chastise him, seconds passed. Nothing happened. No blade came into his side nor pressed into his throat. Not a word was uttered by anyone around him, though Tzui knew they'd be staring at him, ashamed and furious.

A gentle hand brushed his right shoulder. His father's, he didn't doubt. Guessing what was coming, he shoved it farther towards the ground, tearing himself away.

'No!' he cried, his body shaking. 'I won't let you!'

Underneath, he felt the young Alphus press against him, as though sensing his desire to protect them. A few more tense seconds passed in which Tzui braced himself for someone to pull him aside. No other touch followed. The entire universe seemed to hold its breath, unable to predict what was going to happen. He then heard someone shifting alongside him, before his father spoke words that he didn't understand, followed by more sounds of shifting. Soon, Tzui realised his father had sent the other warriors away, dragging the two dead Alphus behind them as they left. Tzui prepared himself one last time, awaiting his father's damning verdict.

'Tzui…' his father said, yet this only fuelled Tzui's resolve, making him tense his body.

'Why?' he demanded. 'Why did we do this to them? They were a family! We're running from those monsters, yet we do this to the Alphus?'

Tzui snivelled, then began sobbing, weeping more than he ever had done in his entire life. Alongside the strange feeling that pulsed from within, he imagined the pain the young Alphus must have felt, the anguish of losing both father and mother as a child. He imagined one of the Infested killing his father, picturing a horrifying beast with many clawed limbs carving him apart with little effort.

'I don't want to lose you like they lost their mother and father…' he said, half confused as to why he was saying it in the first place. 'I'm scared. I have these strange feelings inside of me. Even now they're telling me I'm doing the right thing, even if you could pull me away. I don't understand it, but it's telling me this is wrong. I had to do this.'

Heaviness enveloped his mind, a pressure that made him tense in pain while the feeling within sung with joy. Such conflicting emotions only added to his confusion, making it hurt so much worse as he shook his head.

'I'm not worthy to be leader,' he said. 'I'm not worthy of being your son…'

His father's hand caressed his shoulders once again, not making any move to pull him away. It was a touch of warmth so strange to Tzui that he couldn't help but look up, his vision blurred by his own tears. There was nothing that could have prepared him for what he experienced next.

The sight of his father weeping, as dismayed as he was.

'Tzui,' his father repeated, moving one of his hands to caress Tzui's chin, smiling while still weeping. Unsure what to do, Tzui rose, revealing the Alphus, which quivered in fear. He lowered his hands and stroked them reassuringly.

'I won't let you kill them,' he said, surprised at how determined he sounded despite himself. Yet, that surprise was nothing compared to the surprise he felt when his father nodded in acknowledgement.

'Then something else will, Tzui,' his father said, returning a more level gaze. 'You must understand this if you are to survive.'

Tzui knew it was a fair point, and he acknowledged that with a faint nod. For the next couple of minutes, the two of them continued to sit silently, stroking the young Alphus while Tzui marvelled at how soft their fur was. Regardless, he knew his father was right. If they released the young Alphus and left them to fend for themselves, they'd be lucky to last a couple of hours at most. He understood that even if he saved the two Alphus it wouldn't change the fact that his father and, indeed, his people would continue to hunt them.

Then why did I do this? he wondered, gazing into the innocent blue eyes of the Alphus as they regarded him. *Why did I act in this way? And why does it feel right?*

The strange feeling within stirred again, giving him a sense of clarity that enabled him to return his father's level gaze with one of his own.

'I may not understand the ways of our world as you do, Father. But I cannot watch you kill these young Alphus. I cannot watch you kill or harm another creature. I will accept your punishment for what I've done today, but I know in my heart that I've done the right thing.'

He lowered his gaze and focused his attention back towards

the Alphus, smiling. They were relaxing, seeming to regard him as though he were their tentative mother. They even started making their strange sounds, reminiscent of someone blowing their nose, through their tiny trunks. Tzui laughed, forgetting himself, losing himself in the innocence of the moment. His father moved again, positioning himself cross-legged, his back straight. His hands rested on his knees, and he appeared to be contemplating something.

'Liagnis would not hesitate for a moment before taking them,' he murmured, reaching forward with one hand and allowing one of the Alphus to sniff it. 'Neither would Tshunus. Everything must die, Tzui. Tell me, why should we make another choice when their fate is decided?'

Tzui considered that for a moment. As he intentionally sought out the feeling within, an answer came to him.

'Because we are not the Infested,' Tzui said, allowing the words to settle as he locked eyes with his father. 'Yes, they and the Liagnis and Tshunus wouldn't hesitate, but that's because they cannot think like us. We must be better. We must act better.'

Tzui watched his father then, waiting to hear his response. After a few moments of consideration, a smile emerged on his father's lips. He shook his head and then reached towards the Alphus and began stroking them.

'No, Tzui,' he said. 'We cannot be better. Your mistake is believing that you and our kind are the same when we are not. Our kind can only comprehend so much, but you – you think differently from us. You speak words that could only come from the spirits. You have always been this way, Tzui. That's why I've always known that you are destined for something greater: something beyond our kind and Rakshi.'

His father rose to his feet, making Tzui look up and admire the courageous figure who stood before him. His father was his hero, but he now understood he would never grow up to become him. Unable to help himself, he looked away, feeling ashamed.

'Tzui,' his father then said, drawing Tzui's gaze back to him as he stood tall with pride. 'Do not be ashamed of what you are. However, it is for that reason that when we return to the others, you must understand that I need to become our leader again. I must continue to act in ways that are fitting of our kind. This means I will have to punish you, Tzui. I will have to declare you unworthy of becoming our next leader. This is a sacrifice for our people. Soon you too will have a choice to make. All great things require sacrifice. Remember that your destiny is separate from ours. One day, you will change not only Rakshi but also other worlds within Odia.'

His father paused then, smiling.

'Never forget this, my son. All great things require sacrifice. Never forget that I will always love you…'

He then turned and gestured for him to follow, prompting Tzui to rise to his feet as the Alphus stirred.

'We'll bring them with us. Tonight, I want you to have another discussion with Elder Fyr.'

6

Realisation

'I remember…' Tzui said with a haunting sense of clarity, raising both his hands and looking at them, trying to rationalise what he had done.

I had forgotten what the feeling within had compelled me to do. I allowed my anger and rage to turn me into the monster I never wanted to be.

Tzui stared towards the horde, now seeing nothing but terrified Infested, quivering before him as the young Alphus had once done.

'What happened to my memory?' he asked aloud, confusion rising inside him. 'Who are you protecting?'

Tzui didn't expect them to answer. When he stepped forward, they uttered a shriek, which warned him away. He understood now that they weren't 'monsters', despite their monstrous appearance. Whatever they were protecting, they were willing to die for it. Tzui contemplated this while considering his memories, the strange feeling within emerging once again, a speck of light amid a fog of darkness. The other feeling writhed at his emotions, attempting to force him to continue with the slaughter. He ignored those impulses, struggling against himself while doing so.

I must be better, he told himself in his mind. *I will not become a monster. I will not allow myself to become corrupted.*

He glanced at his father's sword, which was still attached to his side, and reached for its hilt. Upon attempting to remove it, Tzui discovered that the skin on his Odian armour moved with it, as though it were permanently attached to him. Pain engulfed him as he tried to withdraw it, his body shaking in agony while he emitted another shriek of his own.

Why won't you let me use it? he wondered, still straining to draw it from his body. Inside, his instincts stirred, reluctant to release the blade.

You will use it to kill them. his instinct growled. *Destroy every one of them.*

'No… I won't…' Tzui growled back, tightening his grip around the hilt, which increased the pain. 'I will not give in.'

Then, you shall not have it… his instinct replied, prompting Tzui to stop as he loosened his fingers, glancing at the sword, amazed.

'It's you… isn't it?' Tzui asked aloud. 'You are not me, not my genuine emotions. You're the one that's been telling me to kill them, fuelling my rage and my hatred towards them, using my fear and my loss of memory to—'

Tzui stopped himself, realising something that sent a shiver through his body.

'You're the one who's taken my memories, aren't you? But why? Why do you want me to slaughter them? When you're obviously one of—'

I am not one of them! his instinct screamed, fuelling another spike of rage within Tzui, an emotion he forced himself to control while regarding the Infested.

'Tell me, what are you? An Anubian?'

The instinct, whatever it was, didn't answer. Tzui nodded to himself in acceptance.

'I will learn the truth,' Tzui said. At that, something stirred within him. He reached for the hilt of his father's sword again, this time grabbing it in both hands before he attempted once more to draw it away from his body. At once, the pain came flooding back.

What are you doing? his instinct said, incredulous.

'Showing them I'm not their enemy,' Tzui said, then grunted, pulling as hard as he could to free the sword. His skin that covered his Odian armour stretched and pulled agonisingly, compelling him to unleash another scream. He fell to his knees, refusing to release his grip.

I... am not... your enemy... Tzui told the instinct. *This is who I am.*

I know... his instinct replied. *That's why I'm afraid of you.*

Despite his body screaming at him to stop, he kept going, kept pulling as tendrils snapped. Within his armour, he gritted his teeth, straining with all his might to pull the sword free.

Why are you doing this? his instinct asked. *Why do you put yourself through this? Why is it so important that you understand?*

'I think you already know why.' Tzui said, still writhing in pain. He decided he would not entertain any more questions. Inside him, the strange emotion was growing stronger with each second that passed, further strengthening his resolve. With it, he felt he could withstand anything. With it, he felt like the Odian he was meant to be.

'I will be better!' Tzui screamed, and the sword ripped free from his side. Upon its release, he dropped it onto the floor, panting as he looked up to see the horde approaching him. They seemed more curious than afraid, especially one with mismatched limbs and a stooped posture. Staring at it, it became clear to him that the creature had once been an Alphu, its small trunk reaching towards him as he extended his right hand to it.

'We are not so different, are we?' he asked the creature, stroking its face like he had stroked the young Alphus while hunting with his father. Remembering that day and what his father had told him, he smiled.

'What about you?' Tzui asked the instinct, peering at the beautiful warm sky. It did not surprise him when the instinct didn't reply, though something arose from it, a sense of contemplation. As he turned his gaze towards the rest of the horde, seeing Liagnis, Tshunus, and more of Rakshi's other creatures in their new forms, a thought rose within him.

'Something made us into these forms. Something brought the Infestation. That's what you were all trying to protect us from, wasn't it? You weren't trying to destroy or infect us. You were trying to ward us away, never realising that by doing so you were spreading it. It came from something. Something close. Either way, we are all responsible for our actions – including you, whatever you are inside my head. Know that I will discover the truth. You do not have to fear me.'

Yes, I do, the instinct replied. *You do not understand what I've done.*

'Then tell me', Tzui said, now finding himself surrounded by calm and peaceful Infested. 'Give me back my memories.'

Not yet, the instinct said. *I don't know if I can trust you.*

'Allow me the chance to show you,' Tzui said. 'Tell me, what were they keeping us away from?'

The truth... Continue on your path forward. I shall judge whether you are worthy to discover that which compels you most.

'Then we will face it together,' Tzui said, glancing at the Infested he was stroking before reaching to pick up his father's sword. He rose, taking a moment to regard the rest of the Infested around him, now staring at him as though he were their leader.

'Meet me there,' Tzui said to them. 'Meet where it all began.'

Without even thinking, he launched himself into the canopy above, his instincts urging him to reach out and grasp the nearest tendril. He looped around it, using it and his momentum to launch himself even higher. Before he could even question what he was doing, he used the surrounding overgrowth to continue his ascent, leaping between the trees, tendrils, and vines.

Tzui marvelled at his newfound strength and agility, which, coupled with his enhanced senses, made his movement so much faster and more accurate. He felt himself trusting his instinct more while he moved, swinging himself from tree to tree and tendril to tendril. Everything around him grew brighter with sunlight, as the overgrowth thinned the higher he climbed. He chased after the sky, consumed with the desire to reach it, marshalling all of his built-up momentum and reaching for a loose tendril. Then, he swung in an upward arc, rushing towards a gap in the overgrowth.

Tzui broke through it then, to the apex of the most magnificent sight he had ever encountered: the world of Rakshi beneath him. For a single moment of clarity, everything slowed. He regarded the overgrowth that made up so much of his world, witnessing its beauty, a synthesis of emerald and crimson plant life, connected by streaks of violet tendrils. The sky above him was a vast open space, a gentle blue intertwining with slashes of maroon. Inside his Odian body, Tzui's jaw dropped in amazement; he wondered if this was the Rakshi Liagnis saw every day.

Oh Iri...You would've loved this.

He descended, heading towards the sea of overgrowth until his body plunged right into it. His feet somehow found a thick tendril to land on, halting his momentum for a few seconds before launching him away again of their own accord. He allowed his instinct to carry him, traversing his world in a way that no other creature could. Inside, he marvelled at the power he now possessed, the power of an Odian.

I am one of Odia's chosen, he remembered. *That is why we must work together, whatever you are.*

Inside, he felt his instinct's scepticism alongside tinges of its own fear. It was, he understood now, an entity of its own.

What happened to you? he asked, watching as his body continued to rush through the overgrowth.

I was turned into a monster, his instinct admitted. *But not before one of you betrayed me...*

'One of me?' Tzui asked. 'You mean another Rakshian?'

No. I mean one of those who represent Odia's Virtues...

Upon hearing those words, Tzui stopped on a tree, pain travelling through his mind as he worked to search through the fog that shrouded it. He reached towards his head.

'Virtue... Where have I heard that?'

His mind strained as he considered that, then he saw something he didn't think was possible on Rakshi: a great chasm of soil that was void of any plants or wildlife. Instead, it contained a large glimmering silver object shaped in an oval.

'What is that?' Tzui asked aloud.

It is where the Infestation began in your world, the instinct replied. Tzui stepped off the tree and dropped around fifty feet, landing without pain despite having jumped from such a great height.

That's good to know, he thought, stepping towards the vast chasm of soil, turning his attention to the silver shape that lay within the crater.

It's a ship, he realised, though he wasn't sure how he knew that. He had seen nothing like it before, yet a part of him understood it to be true. All around him, more Infested converged upon the site, halting any move to attack him once they recognised who he was.

'There's so much I still don't understand,' he said as he approached the chasm.

You will do soon enough, his instinct said, *for that is the Virtue that compels you. I can see that now.*

'What do you mean?' Tzui said. 'What can you see?'

What Fyr saw in you, along with your father and Iri.

'How do you know about them? What are you?'

I was there, Tzui. I was there when they realised what you are... An Anubian...

Another memory returned to him.

7

The Virtue Of Truth

Tzui had waited until Iri and everyone else was asleep before rising, tiptoeing through the sleeping Rakshians, which provoked shame within him. His father had declared to them his failure during the rite of passage, and that he would not become the next leader of their kind. Only Iri had moved to comfort him, a gesture that he appreciated. His father had made quite the spectacle of his declaration, but inside Tzui understood that the man speaking to his people was not his father. His father had been the one who had shown him love and understanding, the one who had claimed his destiny was beyond even Rakshi.

'All great things require sacrifice.' His father's words echoed in his mind as he approached Elder Fyr, whom he could see watching the stars from his seat on a pulsing tendril.

What is it you know about me? Tzui wondered, nervous at the thought that something terrible was being kept from him. Considering this, he paused, wondering what the Elder was thinking. Then, although Tzui had made no sound, the Elder turned and smiled at him.

'Ah, young Tzui. To what do I owe the pleasure of this visit?'

Tzui steadied himself before answering. He had rehearsed his first words in his mind.

'You knew what would happen when I undertook the rite of passage, didn't you?' he said, watching as the Elder's smile grew. Fyr held the expression for a couple of seconds, saying nothing before breaking his gaze and returning it towards the canopy, prompting Tzui to look up and do the same. High above, the stars in the sky burned in a series of thousands of little fires.

'You know, young Tzui, I have spent many nights looking up towards the stars, dreaming of what lay beyond them. During such moments, Odia looks so beautiful. I will miss these nights… Yet, I find peace in knowing that one day, one of us will reach up towards those stars and clasp the Void within their grasp. I find solace in knowing you will be the one to seek the truth he wouldn't tell me…'

Fyr returned his gaze to Tzui while maintaining his smile. Despite the impulse to question what the Elder meant, Tzui stayed silent. Fyr's expression remained unchanged.

'Will Iri be joining us?' he asked.

For a fraction of a second, Tzui frowned, wondering if this was a distraction.

'No,' Tzui said, deciding to play along with whatever the Elder was doing. 'I waited until everyone was asleep.'

'Everyone except me,' Fyr corrected, his eyes glistening. 'She cares about you, Tzui, almost as much as you do about her.'

Tzui said nothing. He didn't think it was a secret among his people. Of course, many of them would wonder who would marry him now, especially after today's humiliation. Much to his own surprise, he found himself not caring. It didn't diminish his love for her.

'Yes,' Fyr continued, 'sometimes you just know when two are to become one.'

Fyr's expression changed then, becoming more sombre, possessing more gravity. He looked as though he had terrible news to convey. Tzui had to resist the growing anxiety urging him to probe.

'Yet, that is not the bond that awaits you, young Tzui...' Fyr said, his voice trailing.

'What do you mean?' Tzui asked.

'Search within your heart, young Tzui,' the Elder replied. 'I know you feel it. I have seen the way you regard your father's sword. I have seen the way you act when your heart stirs, compelling you to question and seek truth. Tell me, what truth does your heart compel you to seek now? What truth can you see beyond the words I am speaking?'

Tzui broke away his gaze from Fyr, trying to consider what he was saying. Trying to understand.

He wants me to search for truth... Within you. Tzui thought, closing his eyes and allowing the feeling within to rise. Maintaining this intention, he could feel it envelop him, reaching into every part of his soul. It sang in much the same way it had sung before his father, its truths beaming like the sun.

'You and Father both knew what I would do during the hunt,' Tzui repeated, glancing behind to the sleeping form of Iri, who was cuddled up alongside the two young Alphus. 'You both knew that I would move to protect them.'

'We did,' Fyr confirmed. 'And that was why I asked your father to take you on the rite of passage, young Tzui. We both knew what you would do. Someone not of this world told me long ago that someone like you would come. As you grew, I realised what you were. I told your father then, and we have kept the truth from you ever since. Your father and I both believe that the horde's arrival is no coincidence.'

The words echoed his father's, among so others that Tzui wished to question. Yet, one question seemed more important.

'What am I, Elder Fyr?'

It was then that Fyr's smile returned, warm and caring. The warmth stirred the feeling within to sing once again, blossoming like the glowing overgrowth around them.

'You are you, young Tzui. Do not consider the differences between us a bad thing. It is who you are. You have a gentleness that makes you love this world and its creatures. It is this caring nature that has enamoured Iri of you. Like I and your father, she can feel your heart and your love for her, and it is for that reason that she is yours. Inside, you ignite the same feelings of love within her. You see, young Tzui, this is your gift. Your care gives you compassion. Your compassion makes you love. It is your love that then compels you to question. These things make you what you are. These things come from the Virtue that lies within your soul, the feeling that guides your every step.'

'You mean that this feeling means something?'

'Yes, young Tzui. The feeling that guides your soul only exists within a special few, those who have been touched by Odia herself. This Virtue defines who you are and the actions you decide to take. For you see, young Tzui, your Virtue brought you to me today. Your Virtue is why you ask the most difficult of questions. Your Virtue enables the bond to be made.'

'And… What is my Virtue?' Tzui asked. 'What is this "bond" you keep mentioning?'

'Search within yourself, young Tzui,' Fyr replied. 'You know the answer.'

Tzui closed his eyes once again, searching within for the answer, for the truth. It was when he considered the latter that everything became obvious to him, prompting him to open his eyes in surprise.

'Truth…' he intoned. 'My Virtue is Truth.'

'It is,' Fyr agreed, speaking as though the truth haunted him. 'And now, young Tzui, what truths can you see?'

'I see that you and Father have been preparing me for something, for this "bond" you keep speaking of,' Tzui replied, before his eyes widened in realisation. 'To an Odian…'

Stunned, he parted his lips, watching as Fyr's expression didn't change.

'There is no temple, is there?' Tzui asked, feeling disbelief rise. 'There is no Odian to find. It's here, isn't it? It's in the sword father carries, the one he found among the Infested… That is our Odian, but he cannot summon it. It needs someone to bond to… Someone with—'

'A Virtue,' Fyr confirmed. 'Yes. It needs someone like you, young Tzui. Only a few can possess a Virtue. A Virtue makes a person something more, something that possesses their own name.'

'An Anubian…' Tzui said. 'That's what an Anubian is, isn't it? That means—'

'The battle between Anubians and Odians is not one that takes place on the outside. It is a battle that takes place within. The corruption that I spoke of – it is the difference between the choices you make as an Odian. To become the hero you are meant to be, or to become one who uses their power for selfish means.'

'And that's what you've been trying to teach me', Tzui said. 'Because before I can bond with it…'

'There must be a sacrifice.'

Fyr paused then, attempting to keep his smile.

'This is a decision only you can make, young Tzui. Only you can choose to follow your heart. You must choose your own fate.'

'Yet, you already know my decision,' Tzui said, noticing a tear falling down his cheek as a rueful smile emerged on his lips.

'Yes, young Tzui,' Fyr agreed. 'Because we understand who and what you are. You are more than us. You are everything we could have hoped to be. You are the one whose destiny is intertwined with the stars above. It is you whom Rakshians will look back upon with pride, long after you are gone. You are our protector, Tzui, the protector of those who cannot protect themselves. You are our Odian...'

Nodding while understanding with new clarity, Tzui rose to his feet, determined.

'Thank you, Elder Fyr, for everything,' he said. 'Tomorrow, we stop running.'

8

Pain

Tzui remembered rushing to Iri afterword, waking her and revealing his feelings for her. Understandably, she had returned Tzui's confession with an astonished look, even if in the deepest part of her heart she had always known. Iri then admitted her feelings for him, and they spent the rest of the night discussing their plans for the future. They talked about marriage and the children they would raise together. The memory now was bittersweet as he held out his Odian hands.

'We both knew...' he said. 'Yet we allowed our childish minds to imagine, to dream, to hope. Even when we both understood that none of it would happen, we still rejoiced in our dreams. That was my first sacrifice, our sacrifice, as friends, as partners...'

Tzui lowered his hands, looking up to regard the gleaming ship that lay in the centre of the chasm, understanding.

'You withheld my memories,' he said to the instinct, which he now understood was his Odian. 'You wanted me to hate the Infested, to blame them for what happened. You didn't want me to see the truth behind them, and the truth within myself.

Yet even now, I know there's still one more memory that you're keeping from me, the fate that befell my kind when I bonded to you.'

His Odian stirred then, without trying to fuel him with rage and hatred. Instead, confusion and apprehension rose. Tzui smiled, remembering the moment he had shared with his father and the Alphus. Tzui moved his left hand to his right forearm and stroked it – a gesture that brought new feelings from his Odian, longing crossed with fear.

'You're in so much pain,' Tzui said, continuing to stroke his arm. 'All you know is hurt and betrayal. Your last Anubian – they betrayed you, didn't they? They did something to you, and now you question whether you can trust me. I know this because you're giving me back my memories. I understand new terms and concepts. That's how I understand this to be a ship, alongside what it does...'

Tzui paused, allowing his Odian a moment to stir. Inside, hope emerged from it, a small flicker of light that battled against fear.

'We must work together,' Tzui said. 'I am not one of the corrupted. I seek to uncover the truth behind these creatures, behind the Infestation. Help me discover the truth, my Odian. Help me live in accordance with my Virtue...'

His Odian body quivered as sorrow and pain overwhelmed him, so much so that he couldn't help but fall to his knees and weep.

'I am here for you...' Tzui said, trembling, moving his arms so that he wrapped them around his body, around his Odian's body. 'Whatever happened to you, show me. Release your pain, my Odian. You do not have to bear it alone anymore.'

His body quivered once again.

I want to trust you, his Odian said. *But I'm afraid of what you'll do once you discover the truth.*

'We can face it together,' Tzui said, unable to control himself as he slipped away from his own body, feeling his Odian taking control.

No! his Odian cried. *I can't do this!*

It's alright... Tzui said softly in his mind. *We will face it together.*

As though triggered by his words, a new vision came to Tzui.

His body was restricted, bound to a cold hard surface while a blinding light restricted his sight. Strange shapes danced around him. They spoke and mumbled words that were at first unfathomable to him. Tzui focused on them, pulling his eyes away from the light. Moments went by, and one shape stepped forward, leaning towards his face. He watched something extend from it, an object that looked small and pointed. Before he could ask what it was or what was happening, he felt it stabbing into his arm, bringing with it pain and an uncomfortable shifting. His body convulsed, his skin crawling with what felt like a parasite.

'No! Please!' a voice screamed, a voice that Tzui recognised as his Odian's. It had spoken with a strange echo, making it sound distant, like a dream. Yet that didn't make the pain feel any less real. It didn't disguise how powerless and betrayed his Odian felt at that exact moment.

'Why are you doing this?' his Odian cried, struggling to free itself of its bonds.

'I'm sorry, I don't have a choice...' a shape above replied, its voice clear despite echoing sounds around it. 'This is what must be done if Odia is to survive...'

The dream ended with his Odian's scream. Returning to the present, he realised he was lying on the floor, face to face with one of the Infested.

DESTROY IT! his Odian screamed, and for a moment Tzui felt his own hatred return, an urge to kill and destroy. Yet, his Virtue pulsed within, reminding him of what he was. Keeping this in mind, he instead raised his hand and began stroking the Infested on its deformed face, much in the same way he had stroked his arm for his Odian. In response, the Infested leaned towards him, pleased to be touched.

Please... his Odian begged, as though even touching the Infested brought it intense pain.

'Can't you see?' Tzui said, smiling as he watched the Infested close its eyes in satisfaction. 'You both like to be touched. Neither of you want to be monsters...'

Tzui paused. His Odian was listening.

'Can't you see how similar you both are?' Tzui continued. 'How much pain and suffering you both endure? Neither of you asked for this. Neither of you asked to be infected by the Infestation. Both of you suffer for it.'

Tzui pushed himself onto his feet, still looking at the Infested creature and wondering what it once had been. By its temperament, it reminded him strongly of an Alphu. When he considered this, he realised something that should have been obvious.

'This isn't your true form, is it?' Tzui asked, knowing the answer. 'You are not the Odian of Rakshi.'

No... I am not, the Odian admitted, sounding devastated. *As I showed you, I bonded with another Anubian, who betrayed me while somehow keeping me in my armour form while separating. He subjected me to his experiments. He injected the Infestation into me, turning me into this...*

'He was one of the corrupted...' Tzui finished for him.

Yes, his Odian confirmed. *He tricked me into believing that he represented his Virtue, that he wished to save Odia from something. Yet, no sooner did he coerce me to bond with him than he began his experiments. He betrayed what an Anubian is, the essence that binds us together. That is why I took your memory, made you succumb to my anger and hated. I wanted to hurt you in the same way I wanted to hurt him and his Infested monsters. I...*

It trailed off, and Tzui nodded, its hesitation and pain engulfing him once more. In response, he moved to stroke his forearm again, as the pain intermingled with longing.

'I will not betray you,' Tzui said. 'I will not throw you aside. Even if we find my world's Odian, I will find another Anubian to bond with them.'

You don't know me, his Odian replied. *You still don't know the truth of what I've done, the true extent of how far I allowed my hatred to consume me...*

'It doesn't matter,' Tzui said. 'My Virtue, that which guides my soul, is telling me you are my Odian, and that I am your Anubian. We are one, and we shall become who we are supposed to be.'

Still, he felt scepticism from his Odian, along with doubt and anguish.

Will you feel the same way once you understand? his Odian asked, sounding as though it were asking itself. Tzui left it alone, striding forward to place his hand on the ship, feeling a vibration reverberate through it. A whooshing sound followed, accompanied by another loud vibrating hum, while deep-sapphire lines emerged all around the ship. Tzui stepped back and glanced at the Infested creature, which regarded him with a docile look. By the time he returned his attention to the ship, a powerful wind had begun swirling around his body. After a couple of seconds it faded away, leaving the ship floating in a gentle bobbing motion.

'This is incredible,' Tzui said.

'Unit 39067 activated', a female voice said from the direction of the ship. 'Thrusters are at 5% capacity.'

In response, Tzui twisted his head. He could sense remnants of memory and understanding from his Odian, but to Tzui, the ship might as well have been speaking another language. He opened his mouth to ask the ship a question, but it spoke again.

'I do not advise another course of interplanetary travel,' it said, 'at least until I've been refuelled. However, if you wish to circumnavigate this planet, my calculations suggest we could complete 2.7653 rotations. How do you wish to proceed?'

Tzui didn't know what to say. He decided to ask the only question that popped into his head.

'Can you understand me?' he asked.

'I can speak up to 4,748 different languages, dialects, and accents,' the ship replied, sounding annoyed by the question. 'I doubt yours is beyond my vocabulary, Master.'

'Master?' Tzui replied in bewilderment. 'I barely know what you are.'

A lull followed, the ship seeming unsure how to respond.

'That is… unfortunate,' it said. 'Shall I commence shutdown sequence?'

'No,' Tzui replied, baffled. 'How am I your master? What are you? Where do you come from?'

The ship paused again.

'Initiating shutdown sequence,' it said.

'No!' Tzui barked in command. 'Where is the other Anubian?'

His question was too late. The ship descended, its sapphire

lights fading away alongside the loud vibrating hum. Within seconds it was lying on the surface. Tzui shook his head in disappointment.

'That went well…' he muttered, contemplating.

'Did it see you and think it was me?' he asked his Odian, but it didn't answer. There was something else it wasn't telling him; he felt it. Yet, rather than pursue the matter, he wondered how the ship could even carry the Infested with it. It wasn't large enough to carry a horde.

'Something brought the Infestation to my world,' Tzui repeated from before, feeling his Virtue pulse within him once again. 'Something must have started this…'

He looked up from the chasm and saw more Infested making their way towards him. Unlike before, no shrieks or roars accompanied them. Instead, they seemed as calm as the one standing alongside him.

'Unless…' he said, a new idea emerging as he reached towards the Infested at his side. 'Unless the Infestation corrupted you after this ship's arrival, and all of you are from Rakshi…'

He glanced towards the ship again, then stared at his hands, nodding his head. Understanding.

'It was you, wasn't it?' Tzui asked, as a churning sensation in his stomach came from his Odian. 'The ship didn't bring the Infestation with it; you did. Your Anubian brought you here, and you unleashed your Infestation upon my world.'

I want to trust you, but I'm afraid of what you'll do once you discover the truth, his Odian had said before showing him its vision – the vision of what its previous Anubian had done to it. Considering that, everything made sense.

'Your Anubian – it came here to search for our Odian, then found it and finally discarded you. You turned yourself into the sword and unleashed the Infestation before my father found you. It was your Anubian who brought all of this upon us...'

Guilt and shame rose from his Odian, confirming this to be true.

'So, where is he?'

Tzui heard something land on top of the ship, drawing his attention. There stood the Odian of Rakshi.

'It wasn't supposed to be this way...' A male voice emerged from a female-like form.

Inside, his Odian radiated nothing but sorrow and agony.

That's what happened, Tzui now rationalised. *This was the truth you were afraid that I'd discover...*

No, Tzui, his Odian replied. *As much as this shames me, that was not the truth I was afraid you'd discover. That truth lies within the last memory I've kept from you until now. I am so sorry...*

Then Tzui recalled everything.

9

The Sacrifice

Tzui had woken up before everyone else, regarding where Iri lay along with the others. He had enjoyed every moment of their conversation, as they allowed themselves to imagine the adults they would have become, and the children who would've been theirs.

'I love you, Iri…' he said, knowing that his childhood was on the brink of ending. He did not shed a single tear, nor feel any fear in his heart as he rose. His Virtue, meanwhile, pulsed inside, alongside the shrieks of the Infested that loomed behind them.

It won't be long until they're here, Tzui pondered to himself, looking at his kind for the last time. For a moment, pride emerged from his soul, pride in being Rakshian. He knew they had sacrificed much for him, allowing him to learn what he was alongside the destiny he was to fulfil. He nodded, taking in a deep breath while turning his attention to his father, who was watching him from the other side of the group. Without hesitation, Tzui moved to him, seeing that despite having to keep watch during the night, his father showed no signs of weariness. He was tall and courageous. He was everything Tzui aspired to be when he came of age.

As he drew near, murmuring arose among his people who had awakened, accompanied by sounds of shifting movement. Tzui maintained his focus on his father, and on the black sword with the blazing crimson blade. He felt it waiting, waiting to bond with him, waiting to bond with its Anubian. Considering this, it occurred to Tzui that this was his true rite of passage. This was when he would become a man.

No, that's not true. This is when I become an Odian...

Tzui reached his father, and neither said a word at first. His father shifted his gaze towards the sword. The crimson blade seemed to pulse with its own energy, prompting Tzui's Virtue to respond with a similar rhythm of its own. Tzui smiled.

'All this time. The Odian was always here,' he said.

'Yes,' his father replied. 'When I held it, I heard it whispering to me. It told me that only one who is worthy may gain its power, someone who possesses a Virtue of an Anubian. I knew it was you; Elder Fyr had told me long ago of your destiny. We sought to give you more time – time to question, to understand. To force this upon you would have been selfish. It was and always has been your decision to make, my son.'

Tzui nodded, figuring there was nothing else to say, glancing into his father's eyes. His Virtue pulsed more, telling him it was time.

'I'm ready,' he said, reaching out towards the sword before his father stepped away, his gaze never shifting. Tzui shot his father a questioning look, confused by his action.

'Sacrifice. All great things require sacrifice,' his father said. 'Say it.'

Still confused by what his father was doing, Tzui frowned.

His father remained unmoved, unwilling to go ahead unless Tzui spoke the words. Meanwhile, Tzui's Virtue throbbed more than ever before. Tzui pulled his hands away and straightened himself. His people moved to surround them in a circle, their resolve fuelling him as he regarded his father.

'All great things require sacrifice,' Tzui said, drawing a nod from his father, who reached out to the sword, unsheathing it.

'No matter what happens. No matter what faces you in the future. You will remember these words, my son. They are the words that define us as Rakshians, and we shall never yield when circumstance compels us. We shall never crumble. We shall never fall. Not until Odia strangles our last breath. We shall remember these words. We shall live under their wisdom. As an Anubian, as one of Odia's chosen, you shall swear to uphold the Virtue that compels you. The Virtue that shall bond you to this Odian. You shall swear to always represent this gift, to defend those who cannot defend themselves. This is what it means to be leader, my son. These are the words my father passed on to me before I became leader of our people. These are the words I now pass onto you, Tzui.'

He stepped towards Tzui, spinning the sword in his fingers while raising it into the air, then plunging it deep into the ground between them. Kyri then stepped away, extending his arms towards those who were closest to him, taking in their hands. Soon, the others followed, forming a ring around Tzui and the sword. Even Iri, moving with the young Alphus by her feet, formed part of the ring. The only one who hadn't joined was Fyr, whose own face had taken on a proud expression, glancing between Tzui and the morning sky.

'This is our sacrifice,' he said, speaking with gravity. 'As Rakshians, we sacrifice to Odia herself! We do this so that our son, young Tzui, may gain the power to protect others. We make this sacrifice so that Tzui may pursue the Virtue that courses in his heart, the Virtue that deems him worthy of harnessing the power of the Odians. The Virtue of Truth!'

'The Virtue of Truth,' his people chimed. The neon crimson blade of the sword glowed even brighter, responding. Its hilt started shifting as though an insect were scurrying within it, before opening up like a monstrous flower. Before Tzui even knew what was happening, it latched itself onto him, sending a wave of nausea through him that almost made him to fall to his knees, his vision blurring. Inside, something meshed with his Virtue, another presence intermingling with it until it appeared to swallow it whole.

Replacing it with the sounds of shrieking Infested.

Ah... Anubian... An unknown voice spoke from within, filling him with a strange sense of satisfaction. *I have been waiting for you... So I can take my vengeance!*

It coursed with rage and hatred, enveloping him as the sword continued to unwind and unravel, reattaching to his limbs and his body. Tzui dropped to one knee as he struggled. He felt as though he were growing, yet he continued to fight the unnatural force that desired him to yield, to bend, to submit.

I will not bend... he thought to himself, hearing his own voice maturing, growing deeper.

You will bend. The unknown voice replied. *You will make them suffer. You will destroy every one of them. Then we'll hunt for the one who did this to me. We will tear him apart!*

'No...' Tzui whispered, unsure if anyone could hear him. 'That is not what I'm supposed to be... I'm supposed to be a protector.'

You are nothing but a liar! the voice growled as armour formed around Tzui's body. *I will show you. Let's see how loyal you are to your Virtue once everything you love is taken from you...*

When the armour finished encapsulating him, he dropped to his other knee and screamed, a vile shriek that sounded just as monstrous as the Infested. Writhing, something took control of him, forcing him to stagger onto his feet as tendrils formed on his arms and upper body, shaping themselves into tiny blades. The other roared its fury, sending its tendrils towards his kind and piercing them, making them fall one by one. Tzui screamed inside as he watched his Odian carry out its bloody work.

Then he had forgotten. His Odian had stripped away the memory of the moment while leaving the emotions of loss and hatred within Tzui, who knew the horde was drawing closer. It was coming for him as he looked at the corpses, at the fallen bodies of those he had once loved.

'Sacrifice. All great things require sacrifice...' he remembered his father saying. Tzui hadn't understood why he remembered those words.

Not until now.

10

The Odian Of Rakshi

'No,' Tzui gasped, finding himself weeping as he looked at his hands once again.

It was you... It was you who took control of me. It was you who slew my kind.

Tzui's body quivered, his Odian's fear palpable because of this realisation, unsure of what he was going to do. Tzui felt his Virtue burning within him, screaming a truth that he couldn't deny as he gazed towards the other Odian. It floated in the air just as the ship had. Its feminine body possessed violet legs with thick thighs and a neon-green upper torso. Its head was a deep black, with etchings that gave it a face with no mouth or nose. It stared at him with light-blue eyes, while at the back of its head, small black tendrils formed strands that resembled hair. It was an elegant presence, but not even that could distract Tzui from his Virtue, reminding him of the lessons his father and his kind had passed onto him.

'We made our sacrifice,' he said, moving his left hand to his right forearm, stroking it. 'My people made their choice. I will honour them until Odia strangles my last breath. I will honour them by forgiving you, my Odian…'

Inside, he felt his Odian's astonishment.

You wish to keep me? he said, baffled. *After all I've done?*

'I will not continue the cycle of hatred,' Tzui said, holding his emotions in check. 'You were betrayed, and subject to torture before being thrown away…'

He allowed his hands to fall by his sides, returning his focus to the other Odian.

'By you,' he said, forcing himself to stay calm. 'Because of your greed and cruelty, not only have you manipulated this Odian, but you have stolen Rakshi's. While doing this, you brought a foreign Infestation to my world, ruining parts of it and many innocent creatures. I order you to return Rakshi's Odian to its rightful place!'

The other Odian leapt off the ship and landed alongside him. Its body remained floating in the air, as though gravity held only so much power over it.

'There is so much you do not understand, Rakshian. You have no idea what truths I've discovered. I had no choice. I had to betray him…' he said, speaking in a deep male voice despite his feminine form. 'His memory is fractured, and there is much he cannot recall. To kill me now will spell doom for all of Odia. Besides, you know that my ship can hardly travel, so how do you propose I leave this place? Will you return my Odian to me?'

At once, his Odian body trembled, before Tzui raised his left hand and stroked his right forearm.

'He stays with me,' he said, speaking with finality. 'And you shall return to the stars.'

Tzui stopped stroking his Odian's arm, taking another step towards the other Odian, who didn't so much as move.

'You have hurt this Odian so much,' Tzui said, 'that he's terrified to trust me. Have you anything to say? Have you betrayed your own Virtue so badly that you have resorted to abuse and stealing?'

The other Odian shook its head, disappointed.

'Again, you do not understand what's coming, fellow Anubian,' he said. 'My name is Dallar Sarius, and I come from a planet known as Osiris. My mission is to uncover how Odians can evolve, so they can prepare for what is to come. Please, try to understand, I do not do this for selfish gain.'

He lies, his Odian growled from within, and although Tzui believed his Odian, part of his Virtue couldn't help but ask another question.

'Why?'

'Come with me, and I'll tell you everything,' the other Odian said. At first, Tzui tried to step forward, but he found his body reluctant to do so, his Odian resistant.

It's alright; I do not trust him, Tzui reassured his Odian, feeling the resistance ease. In its place he sensed something emerging from the other Odian, a feeling that it was trying to reach him. Tzui then heard faint sounds of a female whimpering.

He's hurting her, his Odian said.

I know... I can feel it.

A plan formed in his mind.

'Let us make a gesture of faith,' Tzui said. 'Release your Odian, and I will release mine. Let us both talk as Anubians and keep our Odians out of this.'

Tzui felt his Odian's fear of that idea, which prompted him to smile. In a roundabout way, he knew his Odian wished to stay with him, afraid of being hurt again. Rather than contradict him, Tzui maintained his focus. Soon enough, his fellow Odian shook their head.

'No, I don't believe you wish to talk, my fellow Anubian. In fact, I believe your intention is to steal this Odian. I know you are inexperienced, and this gives me an advantage. I would advise you to release my Odian. In return, I promise to undo the damage it has caused your world…'

'By "undoing", you mean slaughter them,' Tzui said, glancing back towards the horde standing on the edge of the surrounding chasm. 'No. I will not allow that. These creatures were once native to Rakshi. I shall carve out a place for them to live.'

Tzui returned his gaze to the other Odian, seeing no response.

'But I have one more question for you. What is your Virtue?'

He waited, watching as his fellow Odian's body language shifted.

'Truth.' it said, sighing, its voice matching its guilt-ridden posture. 'My Virtue is Truth…'

Tzui nodded in understanding. Although he saw the irony behind it, he understood that the lesson he was learning was far more important. He had been descending towards a similar path. As he considered this, he also considered the essence of the Virtues themselves, remembering Fyr's wisdom before he died.

'Then you have allowed your Virtue to become corrupted,' he said.

Without warning, Tzui held out his right hand, allowing his father's sword to form from it. Tzui then leapt forward, landing on top of the other Odian while stabbing his father's sword into its chest. It squirmed and struggled, before relaxing a few seconds later, appearing to accept its fate. Meanwhile, Tzui regarded it in disappointment, lamenting what could have been. At these thoughts, he shook his head.

'I shall never allow my kind's sacrifice to have been made in vain,' he said. 'That is why I swear never to repeat your mistake. I will not betray my Virtue…'

Tzui took in a deep breath before relaxing his grip on the sword, rising.

'Which is why if you ever feel that I'm allowing my Virtue to become corrupted, then you must kill me. Do you understand?' he asked his Odian. Before his Odian could reply, he saw Rakshi's Odian fading away, forming into a dagger with a violet hilt and a black blade. In its wake, it revealed the body of the other Anubian.

It was a strange humanoid creature, its grey-skinned body lean with muscle. Its head was round and hairless, its eyes deep pools of black. Its mouth possessed small teeth. For a moment Tzui stared at the body, contemplative.

That will be my next truth to uncover. To find out your purpose, and why you are experimenting on Odians with Infestation.

Nodding to himself, Tzui reached to pick up the dagger, watching it vanish in his grasp as a sense of vitality and power filled him. He stumbled back a few steps in shock, glancing towards his hands in surprise.

'What just happened?' he asked, while another presence emerged from within, alongside his Virtue and the other Odian.

Oh, don't worry about that, it said in a female soprano voice. She sounded much happier than the other Odian, possessing a distinct personality of her own, one that was joyful and full of life.

Don't worry… she repeated, as though feeling his concern. *You can have it back at any time. Just as long as you say please…*

Tzui frowned, bewildered.

'Has she…?' he asked.

Yes... his original Odian answered, *she has bonded to you as well.*

Indeed, I have, the other Odian confirmed, sounding proud of herself for that very reason. Tzui could feel his other Odian's annoyance as it grumbled.

I dislike this, he said. *She's going to be insufferable...*

Well, you're just mean, she said while Tzui shook his head. He gazed towards the Infested horde approaching them.

There's still so much that I don't know, he realised. *I still don't understand what they are, alongside the Odians. I'm still unsure of my purpose as an Anubian...*

That's ok, Rakshi's Odian replied. *We'll figure it out together.*

'Yes,' Tzui agreed, nodding to himself. 'We will. Tell me, do you have a name, Odian of my world?'

I do, she replied. *My name is Raksun. As you said, I am the Odian of your world, Rakshi.*

'And... what of you?' Tzui asked, directing his question at the other Odian. For a moment he appeared to be refusing to reply, before Raksun tutted.

C'mon... If we're gonna help him find the truth, then at least he needs to know your name, Raksun said, filling Tzui with a gentle prodding from within.

Fine, the other Odian said. *My name is Nidium.*

'Thank you, Nidium.' Tzui turned to face the ship.

'We're going to have to figure out a way to refuel it', Tzui said, folding his arms and turning his attention back to the Infested. 'In the meantime, let's find you a home...'

The End

Also by Kieran McLoughlin

Thank you for reading this novella. Hope you enjoyed it! If you want more, please check out my other work below:

Guardians of Odia: The Bonds of Loyalty
Read the epic first book of the Guardians of Odia series now!

The Void Walker, immortal servant of Odia herself, knows something is wrong in the Odia Universe. The Virtues, the source of the Guardian's power, and the guiding principles of the entire universe, are becoming corrupted. Warped. Lost.

And only the Guardians of Odia, the Odians, can bring them back.

However, the Guardians aren't united, focused on their own worlds and problems. Someone must unite them. Someone must rise and stand for what the Virtues once represented.

And the Void Walker has chosen his champion, the Odian of Osiris, Ero Kalid.

Ero has seen the shift in his own galaxy. His world's mortal enemy, the Gorkas Federation, sweeps across the galaxy, invading and conquering worlds. He knows the Odians must come together to stop them.

But what if the Guardians themselves are becoming corrupted? When war and tyranny threaten the entire Vegeta Galaxy? Ero must unite the other Odians before it's too late. Someone must rise to lead them.

Or else, the corruption will ruin the Odia Universe…